Amazing Ants!

by Renee McCuen

Illustrated by David Hemenway

Worthington, Minnesota

Acknowledgements

Thanks to my daughters for reading and commenting positively on my many, many revisions and to my friends who read and encouraged. Special thanks to Ryan Jacobson for leading me through every step of the publishing process. His input proved to be invaluable.

Credits

Edited by Ryan Jacobson

Logo design by Shane Nitzsche

ISBN: 978-0-9833667-0-6

10 9 8 7 6 5 4 3 2 1

Printed in the U.S.A.

*For my husband, Bob, and
my daughters, Jenny and Leah,
for your patience and encouragement*

—Renee McCuen

Amazing Ants!

Contents

1

STRANGE FORTUNES

Scientists must take risks to learn.

I looked at the strange fortune again. I was with the Sanchez family at our favorite restaurant, Lee's Chinese Palace. Usually my fortune says something like, "Plan your work and work your plan."

I kicked my friend Ester under the table. "What does yours say?" I asked.

She cracked her cookie and pulled out its tiny slip of paper. "It just says *go*."

Mr. Lee stopped by our table. The bald man smiled, wiping his hands on his bright white apron.

"Mr. Lee, Ester and I keep getting goofy fortunes," I told him.

"Goofy? Tell me what they say, Danny."

I dug into my pocket and pulled out my last two fortunes. I also handed him my new one.

Jellyfish and ants are interesting.

Prepare to get wet.

Scientists must take risks to learn.

"Hmm, those are goofy. Ester, what do yours say?" asked Mr. Lee.

"One says *ready*. The next says *get set*. And the last one says *go*."

Mr. Lee nodded thoughtfully. "It sounds like you should prepare for an adventure."

He signaled for us to follow him to the back of the restaurant. We walked through the kitchen and to the storage room. It was stacked with boxes filled with chopsticks, napkins and other supplies.

Mr. Lee pulled a large box down from an overhead shelf. He gave each of us a white paper bag, and then he opened the box. It was packed with wrapped fortune cookies.

"Fill your bags with cookies. I think you're going to need them." He grinned widely.

Ester and I were amazed at our good luck. We reached way down to the bottom of the big box. The cookies rustled against each other as we chose the ones we wanted.

"Wow, thanks Mr. Lee!" I exclaimed.

When our bags were full, Ester and I walked back to our table. We couldn't wait to crack open more cookies when we got home. Maybe one of them would explain why Mr. Lee had said, "Prepare for an adventure."

2

JELLYFISH

Ester and I hurried back to our small apartment building. Ester's parents own the place. My mom has rented from them since I was in kindergarten.

As soon as we got there, we tore into our paper bags. It was really strange. We each opened three cookies, and they all said the same thing.

You don't need a fortune yet.

We tried a few more times during the rest of the day, but the messages were always the same. I went to bed wondering what was wrong with those cookies.

The next morning, Ester and her family brought me to the city aquarium. It was a large building lined with tanks full of underwater plants and animals. Some tanks were so big that they went from the floor to the ceiling. One part of the building even had an underwater glass tunnel to walk through.

Ester and I spent a long time watching the seahorses. They fluttered their fins to move through the water. They swam short distances from plant to plant. The seahorses grasped onto the plants with their tails because they're such weak swimmers. They had to do that so they wouldn't float away.

After that, we found the jellyfish. They glided up and down in the water. Their tentacles gently swayed. The jellyfish were white but kind of see-through. We had to look carefully to see each one.

"Jellyfish are so interesting," I said.

Ester said it too, at the very same time.

All of a sudden, we were inside the tank. We had tentacles. Cool water flowed all around us. I wanted to scream!

But then we were kids again. We were standing by the tank, soaking wet. Ester's dad found us there, dripping. He asked us what happened, but neither one of us answered.

Back at the apartment, I asked Ester about it.

"You must be dreaming, Danny," she answered.

I asked her again, and she covered her ears. I think she wanted to forget. But we had left drippy, wet footprints on the aquarium floor. We needed to change our wet clothes when we got home.

Ester will have to talk about it soon. I've been thinking, and I have an idea called a hypothesis.

3

HYPOTHESIS

I gathered my research books and went out to the front steps. The sun felt warm on my face. Bees buzzed around the bushes.

I thought of my mom. She loves sunny days, but she spends most of them working in a nursing home. At night, she goes to college. She's studying to be a nurse. Lucky for me, Ester's family takes care of me when my mom is gone.

I sat down, thinking about jellyfish, scratching my orange hair. My mom always says, "Danny, your hair is red, just like mine." But once, I held up a carrot while she was fixing her hair. It matched her hair perfectly. Her cheeks turned bright red, but she still says our hair is red, not orange.

The door flew open behind me. Hector, Ester's older brother, raced outside. He stopped when he saw me. "You look serious, Danny. What's up?"

"I'm making a hypothesis."

"That's a big word," said Hector. "Do you know what it means?"

I nodded. "Last year, my third-grade teacher, Mrs. Roos, taught us. A scientist asks questions and makes a good science guess. That guess is called a hypothesis. Once a scientist makes a hypothesis, he tests it to see if it's right."

"Good, so what's your hypothesis?"

I wasn't going to tell Hector that Ester and I turned into jellyfish. He would probably think I was crazy.

"I'm still thinking," I told him.

He shrugged and then sprang off the top step. He accidentally landed on a cricket and squashed it.

Hector picked up his foot and shook it, trying to remove the bug's gooey remains. "Gross!"

He rubbed his tennis shoe against the grass. Then, hooting like a loon, he swung onto his bike. "See you, Danny," he said. "Don't let your head swell from all that thinking." He pedaled down the street and out of sight.

Hector definitely wasn't a scientist. Scientists never say, "Yuck," or, "Gross." Instead a scientist would say, "Interesting," because everything in the world is interesting. Even bug guts.

I settled down with my books again. And once again, the door squeaked open.

4

"INTERESTING"

"What are you reading?" Ester asked.

"I got a book called *The Ant and the Elephant*. Do you want to read it with me?"

Ester plopped down beside me. We took turns reading the story. The elephant helped the ant, and then the ant helped the elephant.

"Ants are amazingly strong," I told Ester. "They are very interesting creatures."

"Don't say interesting!" she screeched.

I picked up my other library books. They were all about ants.

"Did you know that scientists who study insects are called entomologists?" I asked. "An entomologist who studies ants is called a myrmecologist."

Ester glared at me with her large brown eyes. "What's with you? Ants, ants, ants!"

"We need to talk about the aquarium," I said.

"No, I don't even want to think about it," replied Ester. Her long, black braids flip-flopped as she shook her head.

I noticed an ant crawling across the sidewalk. The yard was filled with ant houses—donut-sized mounds of sand.

"Why not?" I asked. "It was interesting."

"Stop saying that," snapped Ester. "We both said that word at the same time. It made the jellyfish thing happen."

I nodded. "That's my hypothesis too. I've tried saying it alone, but it doesn't work."

19

Ester moaned and rubbed her forehead.

"Don't you think ants are interesting?" I asked.

"No," said Ester. "I really don't."

"Come on. I know you're interested. All the mounds have a queen ant, female worker ants and winged male ants. Did you know that?"

"Who cares?" replied Ester.

"Around the end of August, the males and new queens come out from the mounds and fly. They mate. Then the males fall to the ground to die. The queen chews off her wings and digs a tunnel to begin a new colony of ants."

"You won't change my mind," Ester warned.

I wasn't ready to give up. "Did you know ants have been around since the time of the dinosaurs? And I wonder what it looks like inside an ant hill."

Ester stared at one of the mounds in the yard. "Danny," she said, "what if we turn into ants and can't change back? What if we stay ants forever?"

I shrugged. "We turned back into ourselves after being jellyfish."

"I know," she said. "But I'm not sure how we did it."

"Ester, what happened was amazing. I think we were meant to learn about animals. When we find out all we can, we change back."

"Do you really think so?" asked Ester.

"I've been studying ants the last few weeks. I know a lot, but I sure would like to see how it feels to be one. Wouldn't you?"

"I guess so, but we need to stick together. I don't want to get lost in an ant tunnel," she said.

I smiled in agreement. Our talk was going well. I thought it would take longer to change her mind.

5

NEW FORTUNES

"Danny, remember our fortunes?" Ester asked. "One said we would get wet. Another said ants and jellyfish are interesting. Now that we know what they mean, we should open a couple more cookies. Maybe they'll tell us something new."

I had forgotten about the cookies. We ran inside and grabbed our paper bags. Once we had them, we settled back onto the steps outside.

I grabbed a cookie, and Ester did too. We ripped the plastic off and cracked open the cookies.

My fortune worried me a little. It said, *Milk an aphid and feed the queen to become human again.*

I'm glad I read about ants because I know what aphids are. And feeding the queen shouldn't be too hard either.

"What does yours say?" I asked Ester.

"It says to try new foods. What about yours?"

"Milk an aphid and feed the queen." I left out the last part because I didn't want to scare her.

"Milk an aphid? What does that mean?"

I giggled and said, "You know how farmers have cows? Well, ants have aphids—tiny insects. Ants milk them to get their sugary juice."

Ester shrugged. I couldn't tell if she understood or not, but she changed the subject.

"Maybe we should open another fortune, just to be sure we're ready," she suggested.

It was a good idea.

I dug into my bag and pulled out another cookie. My second fortune said, *Be careful of mandibles.*

Mandibles are ant jaws, and they are sharp. This fortune worried me even more than the first.

"Mine says the same thing about trying new foods," noted Ester. "I wonder what kinds of foods I'll be trying." She grimaced. "I am a bit picky about what I eat."

Ester was so busy thinking about food that she didn't ask about my second fortune. That was good. She might change her mind if I let her know about the mandibles.

It was time to test our hypothesis. We stood at the edge of the grass, looking at a small mound of dirt. We grabbed each others' hands and shouted, "Ants are so interesting!"

6

BECOMING ANTS

Nothing seemed to happen.

I stood still, holding Ester's hand. At least,
I thought I was holding her hand, but I couldn't
feel it.

I looked down. My hand was brown and had
claws at the end of it. I looked up. The house was
gigantic, and the mound of sand was huge.

We were ants!

All of a sudden, I heard gasping and choking.

"What's wrong, Ester?" I turned toward her and
saw her brown ant body.

"I can't breathe," she gasped. "I keep opening my mouth, but nothing happens."

"Ester, you're fine. Ants don't breathe through their mouths. They breathe through little holes on their sides called spiracles."

She stopped gasping. "You're right. I'm not running out of air. I think you'd better tell me about these bodies, so I know what to expect."

"All right, stand beside me, and I'll tell you what I know."

It took a little while to get our legs moving. It's awkward walking on six legs when you're used to having two.

As I got a good look at Ester, I burst out laughing. She looked like an ant, but she looked like herself too. Instead of ant eyes, I could see Ester's big brown eyes. Her ant head had black, braided hair. She looked so funny that I couldn't hold it in.

I laughed and laughed. I fell over with my ant legs and antennas wiggling wildly in the air.

"What's the matter with you?" Ester asked. But then she started laughing too. "Danny, you have orange hair on your ant head," she sputtered, rolling on the ground beside me.

After we caught our breaths, we climbed back onto our legs. It was time to tell Ester all about her new ant body.

"Ants don't have bones like people do," I said. "They have a hard outer body called an exoskeleton. The exoskeleton protects them."

Ester nodded.

"Ants have three main body parts: the head, the thorax and the abdomen." I pointed at each part to show her. "The head has compound eyes. Well, ants do, but I guess we don't. The head also has antennas. Ants feel and smell with them."

I clicked my mandibles together. "Ants use their mandibles for cutting, carrying and fighting."

"What about the other parts of the body?" asked Ester.

"Your middle part, the thorax, is where your six legs are attached. The abdomen is the back end of your body."

Ester wiggled her antennas. I could tell she was having fun.

"Are you ready to go into the hill?" I asked.

She nodded her ant head, and off we went.

7

ANT FOODS

I was so excited. Pretty soon, we would find out what an ant tunnel was like. It would be dark in there, but ants have ways of getting around in the dark. I had to tell Ester about the lack of light, and she wasn't going to like it.

Something on a nearby plant distracted me. It looked like a tiny white bulb. It was an aphid.

"Just a minute, Ester. I see something that I want to grab."

I walked up the stem of the plant and came face to face with a ladybug.

"Back off," I told her. "That aphid is mine." I carefully grabbed the tiny aphid in my mandibles and carried it back to Ester. When I found her, she was munching on a large, dead caterpillar!

"What are you doing?" I exclaimed.

"You wouldn't believe it, Danny. Someone left this juicy caterpillar just sitting here. I had to have a taste. I couldn't resist."

All of a sudden, she stopped chewing and looked at me with a sick face. "I'm eating a caterpillar!" she wailed.

"It's okay," I said. "Some ants eat dead insects. It's part of their diet."

"Maybe," she replied. "But I don't." She looked at the aphid I was holding and added, "Are you going to eat that insect? It's still wiggling."

I told Ester that ants don't eat aphids. Some ants take care of aphids. They bring them into their

tunnels and put them on the roots of nearby plants.
The ants clean them and kind of milk them.

"You said that before," Ester remembered. "How
do you milk an aphid?"

"An ant touches the aphid with its antennas. The
aphid gives off a drop of liquid from its abdomen.
The liquid is called honeydew, and it's supposed to
be sweet and nutritious."

"Ugh," replied Ester. "Let's go inside before I
change my mind."

It was time to tell her. "Remember," I said,
"we're going underground. It's like being in the
basement, except with no lights." I prepared myself
for her scream.

"No lights! How do you expect us to get
around? Did you bring a flashlight?"

Don't worry. We'll use our ant senses to find our
way around. Our antennas are so sensitive that they

will make it seem like we can see everything in the tunnel." I thought for a moment before saying, "I just hope we have the same scent as the ants in this ant hill, or else . . ."

"Or else what?" Ester snapped.

"Well, the ants might not like us being here if we don't give off the same scent, or pheromones. We'll know we're safe if they don't want to fight us."

Ester turned and started marching toward the house.

"Where are you going?" I asked.

"There's no way I'm letting an angry ant near me with its sharp mandibles. I'm going home," she said.

It was then that I noticed several ants walking around us. They didn't pay any attention to us.

"Come back, Ester," I yelled after her. "The ants don't mind us being here. We can go in!"

8

THE ANT HILL

"Stay right behind me," I said to Ester. "We'll follow the pheromone trail into the ant hill. I want to find the eggs and larvas and pupas. That way we can see all the stages of an ant's life."

"What's a larva and a pupa?"

"A larva is when an ant egg hatches. The larva doesn't look like an ant. It's more like a hungry, white worm. The adult ants take care of it. They keep it clean and feed it."

"I didn't know that baby ants looked like worms," said Ester.

"That's right," I told her. "Many insects have a four-stage life cycle. First they're an egg, and then they're larva. When they're ready, they turn into a pupa, and at last they're an adult insect."

"Tell me about the pupa," Ester said.

"It's when the insect is resting while its body changes to an adult. Some insects spin a cocoon, and some just look strange. They don't eat or even move very much during this time."

"That's weird, Danny, but interesting. I really want to see— I mean, I really want to feel all of it. Stay close, though. I don't want to lose you."

"I'd like to find the queen too," I added. "She has thousands and thousands of babies, and did you know most of them are females?"

We started slowly into the ant hill. The light disappeared in a hurry. It was so dark that I couldn't see my antennas in front of me.

"Hey, Ester, quit poking me in the bu— I mean, abdomen."

"Sorry," she whispered. "I'm just a little nervous. I wanted to make sure you were still in front of me. Will you keep talking so I can hear you?"

"Sure," I said. "Before I did my research, I thought ants only made tunnels in the ground. But I learned that some ants tunnel into dead trees. Some make their homes in the soft centers of branches. Others don't have a home at all. They gather into a ball when they aren't traveling. They keep the queen, the eggs, larvas, and pupas in the middle of the ant ball to protect them."

Ester laughed. "An ant ball? That's funny."

"My very favorites are the weaver ants. They clamp their mandibles onto leaves and pinch them together. Then they move a larva back and forth along the leaf edges. The larva spins silk, and the silk holds the leaves together like glue. The weaver ants use these leaves to make a nest to live in."

We walked down the tunnel until we came to a chamber.

"This is where the aphids are," I told Ester. "They suck the juices out of the plant roots here. If we touch the aphids with our antennas, we can drink their honeydew."

Milking an aphid was one of the jobs we had to get done. I thought it would be easy, but then I saw a very large ant. She looked like a soldier, and she was guarding the aphids!

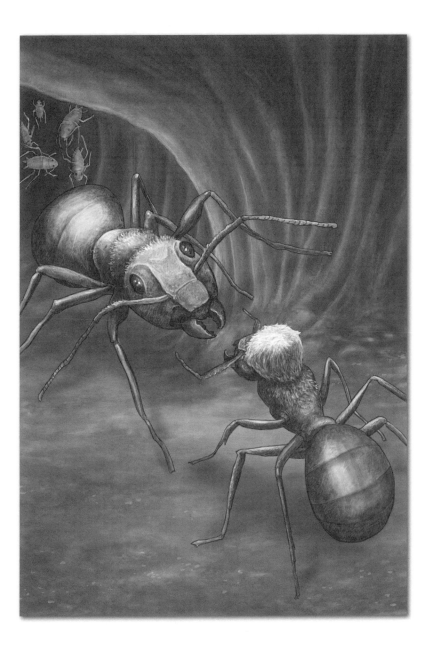

9

MILK AN APHID

I tried to go into the chamber, but the ant wouldn't move. She must have sensed something different about me. I heard her mandibles clicking.

"Danny, don't go any farther," said Ester. "She won't let you in." Ester didn't know we needed to go inside, or we'd never become human again.

I moved closer. The ant swiped at me with her sharp jaws.

"Hey, leave my friend alone," shouted Ester. "Let's just leave, Danny," she said to me. "I don't want you to get hurt."

"I don't want to get hurt either, but we have to go in there. That's what my fortune said."

The news left Ester speechless. We stood in the tunnel together, thinking.

At last Ester pointed her antennas at the aphid in my mouth. She said, "Pass that little insect to me. I'll offer it to the guard. Maybe she'll take care of it and put it on some roots. Then we can do our job."

Ester carefully took the creature from me. "You are a wiggly little thing," she said to the aphid.

She bravely stepped forward. "Find a root for this aphid," she instructed the guard ant.

I don't know if the ant understood Ester, but she didn't threaten her. The ant gently took the aphid and moved into a room off the tunnel.

"Wow, you were great!" I exclaimed.

We hurried into the chamber. I reminded Ester that we had to use our antennas to stroke aphids, and then we could suck up their juice.

"Are you crazy?" Ester asked. "I already tasted caterpillar. I think that's enough."

"Honeydew is supposed to be a lot like honey. I'll taste it first."

I touched an aphid, and it released a drop of liquid. I carefully drank it up. Wow! It was sweet and delicious.

"It's really good. I'm not kidding!" I had to have some more.

Ester tried it too. At first, I could tell she was nervous. But then she smiled and said, "You're right, Danny, this is great!"

We ate until we were full. Our ant stomachs were tiny, so it didn't take long.

Once finished, it was time to see the queen. I hadn't been worried before, but now I thought that feeding the queen might be a problem.

There was only one ant guarding the aphids. The queen is always surrounded by lots of ants. Her job is to lay eggs, so she needs plenty of care. If we had this much trouble with one ant, what would happen when we were outnumbered?

10

THE QUEEN

Ester groaned. "I'm so full. I think I might burst. But at least these ant legs work better, now that I'm used to them."

We scurried down a tunnel until we found the queen. Her chamber was crowded with ants doing jobs to help her. Some were moving eggs to another chamber. Some were licking her body to keep it clean. Some were feeding her.

"She's amazing," said Ester. "I'd really like to do something for her, but I'm not sure what."

"Maybe you should feed her," I suggested.

That was our other task. I hoped it would be easier than milking the aphids had been.

"Be careful," I warned. "We should have a plan ready if they decide to attack us."

Ester didn't hear me. She had already stepped up to the queen. I squeezed my eyes shut and waited for Ester to scream. Instead, I heard her telling the queen how beautiful and amazing she was.

Ester touched the queen with her antennas and then shouted, "Sorry!"

She ran to me and started crying.

"What's wrong?" I asked.

"When I got close to her, I was really nervous. I threw up in her mouth!" Ester cried even harder.

I couldn't help it. I started to laugh. "Oh, Ester, it's okay," I said. "You didn't really throw up. Ants have two stomachs. One is for the ant to get the food it needs. The other is called a crop. It's a social

stomach that ants use to feed other ants. When animals spit up food from their crops, that's called regurgitating."

Ester smiled and wiped away her tears. "I guess some ants never leave the ant hill," she said. "They work hard all the time. Someone has to feed them."

"That's right. Ants use their antennas to let other ants know if they want to be fed. Ants with extra food in their crops feed them by regurgitating food."

Ester beamed. "I fed the queen! I fed the queen! I ate a caterpillar and drank honeydew to help her out. You should feed the queen too, Danny."

"I want to try it, but I think I'll wait to feed the larvas," I told her. "Let's go check them out."

I was glad that we had done our jobs. Being an ant was interesting, but I wouldn't want to stay one forever.

11

BABY ANTS

Our antennas told us where the eggs were stored. We started walking uphill.

"How do these tunnels work?" Ester asked. "Why don't they collapse?"

"Ants use spit to keep them sturdy," I told her. "Plus, hundreds of walking ant legs keep the dirt packed together."

We stepped into the egg room.

"Wow, there must be hundreds of eggs stacked here," I said, amazed. "Look at how well they're cared for, Ester. Let's lick them."

"What? Why would I want to lick an ant egg?"

"The eggs are underground, where it is cool and damp," I answered. "If the eggs aren't licked, they'll get moldy and die."

"We don't want that to happen," agreed Ester. She started licking.

It reminded me of how a mother cat licks her kittens to keep them clean.

After we had licked quite a few eggs, it was time to take care of the larvas.

"Ants lick larvas to keep them clean, but the larvas also need to be fed," I told Ester.

We fed the plump little larvas in the same way Ester fed the queen. Regurgitating felt strange, almost like throwing up.

"You're right," cooed Ester. "They are like little worms. I think they're sweet. Hey, Sweetie, do you want some more food?"

"The pupas are next," I said as we started to another chamber. I sighed to myself, sensing that our adventure was coming to a close.

Each pupa was wrapped in a tight white cocoon. They didn't move at all. I wondered how they got out of the cocoons, but then I noticed an ant gently opening one with her mandibles.

"Let's help get a few out," I said.

We could tell with our ant senses which of the pupas were ready to hatch. We cut open several cocoons to help the adult ants out.

"The ants are so soft," Ester said.

"Their exoskeleton will get harder and darker," I replied. "Pretty soon they'll be working and helping the colony survive."

Finished, we climbed back to the surface. Ester walked out first. I joined her atop the donut-shaped mound, where we waited to become human again.

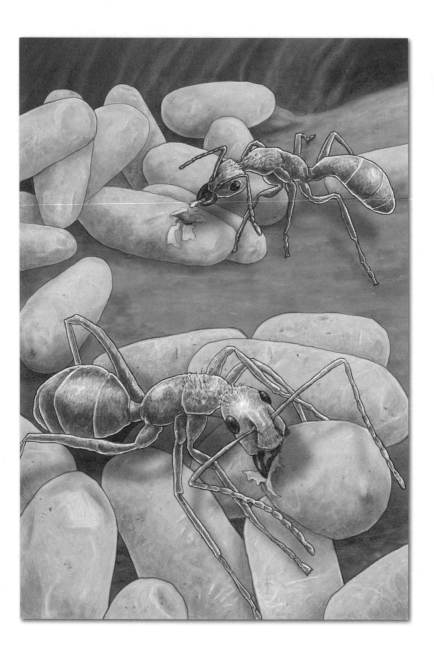

12

THE HUGE FOOT

Ester and I joined claws, ready to change back into kids. But nothing happened.

"Danny, I'm going to be mad if I have to be an ant the rest of my life!" yelled Ester. She stomped her feet.

Suddenly, the sky went dark. I looked up, and I gasped. A gigantic tennis shoe was coming down, right on top of us!

I didn't see how it could miss. We would end up like the cricket that Hector had stepped on earlier today. We would soon be a pile of ant goo.

"Ester, run!" I shouted.

Our ant legs wouldn't work. The foot came closer and closer. It landed on us with all of its weight. For some reason, it didn't hurt.

"Danny, are we dead?"

I didn't feel squished . . . or dead. I looked up again. Ester's brother's foot was on my back—my human back. We were normal again!

"Hola, niños," Hector said, jumping back. "Where did you come from? I didn't see you there." He moved his foot to crush the ant hill.

"Stop, Hector!" screamed Ester. "Those ants never hurt you. Leave them alone!"

Hector looked puzzled. "Okay, okay, when did you decide you liked ants?"

"I think ants are int— um, fascinating. Danny does too," replied Ester.

Hector shrugged his shoulders.

"Mom asked me to tell you it's time for supper," he said. "Did you know you have dirt in your hair and on your clothes? You'd better go clean up."

Hector took off laughing, and we followed him up the steps.

"I hope that we have room for supper after everything else we ate," I said. "I'll go clean up and meet you in a little while."

I headed up to my apartment thinking about the day. But I wasn't just thinking about ants anymore. Don't tell Ester, but I was also thinking that salamanders are very interesting!

Observing Ants

Warning: Don't handle ants. They can have painful bites or stings. Be careful where you sit, too. Sitting on an ant hill can be very uncomfortable!

1. Find an ant hill. Ants are plentiful. You can find ant hills almost everywhere. Take time to observe the ants' movements. You may want to take along a magnifying glass to help with your observations.

2. Some ants like sweets. Bring sugar or small cookie crumbs to place near the ant hill. Watch what the ants do with the crumbs.

3. If the ants don't like sweets, try tempting them with small seeds.

4. Keep a journal of your observations. See what they do when it's rainy, hot or cold outside.

5. Purchase an ant habitat, and watch your ants tunnel and move.

Ant Challenge

How well do you know ants? Answer the questions below, and find out!

1. What do you call a scientist who studies ants?

    a. Anthologist   b. Myrmecologist   c. Geologist

2. What are mandibles?

    a. Ant jaws   b. Ant ears   c. Ant food

3. What does an ant breathe through?

    a. Its nose   b. Its mouth   c. Its spiracles

4. What is the life cycle of an ant?

    a. Egg, pupa, larva, adult

    b. Egg, larva, pupa, adult

5. What is the hard outer body of an ant called?

   a. Skeleton   b. Skin   c. Exoskeleton

6. What is one thing an ant can do with its antennas?

   a. Smell   b. Fight   c. Dig

7. What will an ant do with an aphid?

   a. Eat it   b. Leave it alone   c. Milk it

8. When an ant looks like a little white worm, what is it called?

   a. Pupa   b. Larva   c. Adult

9. What does an ant use to feed other ants?

   a. Its antennas   b. Its crop   c. Its claws

Answers: 1.b, 2.a, 3.c, 4.b, 5.c, 6.a, 7.c, 8.b, 9.b

About the Author

Renee McCuen has enjoyed working with children as an elementary school teacher for 34 years. Her favorite subject is science.

Just like in the story, her students learned to never say, "Gross," or, "Ick." Instead they would say, "Interesting," because everything in the world is indeed interesting.

We have creatures big and small living in our neighborhoods and sometimes even in our houses. Renee hopes *Danny & Ester's Fortunate Adventures* will help you to learn about some of these creatures and to be curious about the others you see.

Renee lives in Worthington, Minnesota, with her husband, Bob, who buys her microscopes and rocks, and listens to all of her "interesting" facts.